D0600422

A Children's Story about Mountain Wildlife

By Sally Plumb
Illustrated by Lawrence Ormsby

Grand Teton Natural History Association

To Glenn and our children, Jenny, Kit and Skye Sally Plumb

Text by Sally Plumb
Technical consultation by Dr. Glenn Plumb
Project coordination by Sharlene Milligan
Illustrations by Lawrence Ormsby
Book design and production by Carole Thickstun
Color separation by Robin Mansanarez, Pioneer of Jackson Hole
Printing coordination by John Batenhorst, Pioneer of Jackson Hole

ISBN 0-931895-25-1 paperback
ISBN 0-931895-26-x hardback

AUTHOR'S NOTE:

PIKA (pronounced *pie-ka*)

Learning to argue with pikas, in their own language, is a treat. After many hours of conversation, the closest imitation of their cry I could reach is: "BEEEEEJE" (pronounced *Bee-jje*).

From this call, I have borrowed the main character's name of "Beejer" (pronounced *Beee-jjer*).

A PIKA'S TAIL

Beejer was born in the spring and the biggest thing about him was his voice. His mother laid him in a warm nest and covered him sweetly with hay.

He was a pika* and he lived high in the mountains.
He had gray-brown fur, short round ears and
a soft white tummy, a small body, four small paws,
but no tail. . . no, not even a small one, I'm afraid.
Oh, how he wanted one! The weasel had one.
Even the marmot had one. But Beejer did not.

* pronounced *pie-ka*

He looked for it. But it was nowhere to be found. He thought someone had taken it. But none of the other pikas had tails. At last he decided that all of the tails were lost. Surely they would come if he called!

So [illegible] is rock and called and called.

"BEEEJE. [illegible]EEEEJE! BEEEEEEJE!"

What a sound he could make! It was a bit like a bark and a bit like a squeak, a bit like a cry and a bit like a peep. It was loud! And it was wonderful!

No tails came, of course.
But what a joy it was to call! And from that day on, the mountain was never quiet.

Beejer lived in a small tunnel, high in a jumble of rock. From his front door he looked over a wide green valley and a rushing stream.

He was not alone on the mountain—not by any means! The marmot and her babies dozed in the sun. The deer grazed in the valley and wandered in the trees. Other pikas scurried about, carrying grass in their mouths.

And, of course, there was the weasel.

His name was Hunter and he lived down near the stream. He was sleek and brown and fast. And he liked to eat mice and rabbits and. . . pikas. Beejer watched him almost as carefully as he watched for the Lost Tails.

Spring soon became summer, wrapping the valley in long, warm days. Beejer grew quickly, as pikas do, and soon he was as big as his mother. "A nice size," Hunter noted as he took a long, cool drink from the stream.

As time went on, Beejer found himself too busy to worry about the weasel very much. He had work to do. Yes, and lots of it. There were tunnels to dig and grass to take, food to store and hay to make.

Pikas do not sleep in winter, you see. Instead they gather enough food to last through the cold time. Beejer wished he were a marmot. They laid in the sun and ate until they were fat enough to sleep all winter long. And the marmot had a fine, bushy tail! It would be better to be a weasel, Beejer decided, thinking about Hunter. How grand it would be to dive and play in the snow! And what a lovely coat Hunter grew for the cold! It was white as snow, with just a tip of black on the tail! Beejer's own coat just got a bit thicker in winter.

Beejer sank his teeth into sweet yellow flowers. He cut them carefully, then laid them in the sun. Turning the plants so they would dry on all sides, Beejer wondered where Hunter was. Working hard all day, he watched carefully for the weasel.

At sunset, Beejer relaxed on his rock. The grass and flowers were cut, dried and neatly stacked. Soon he would have nearly a bushel of hay to eat during the long, cold time ahead.

He called loudly to two pikas nearby. "Beeje!" They answered back. He asked if they had seen the Lost Tails and soon forgot about everything else.

But Beejer would have been smarter to think about weasels, because. . .

Hunter was tired, grouchy, and very hungry, indeed. The noise on the rocks grabbed at Hunter's ears. Pikas again! As one voice piped above the others, Hunter's eyes flew open. He knew that voice. It belonged to Beejer! He crept slowly up the hill.

Beejer sat up and stretched. “BEEEJE! BEEEJE!” he called. He looked around, scratching his ear. Hunter padded across the rocks, silent as a shadow. Beejer sniffed, feeling nervous. The weasel edged on. Closer. . . and closer. . .

Then, just as he was so close that he could see Beejer's whiskers, Beejer squealed and Hunter sprang! You wouldn't think Beejer's fat little body could move so fast! But it could. And it did! Into a crack and Hunter landed on empty rock!

Beejer ran! His paws slipped-pitter-patter across the stone. His heart thumped and bumped against his ribs. Hunter lunged toward him as Beejer dodged for his door. Hurry, Beejer, hurry! Get to your hole!

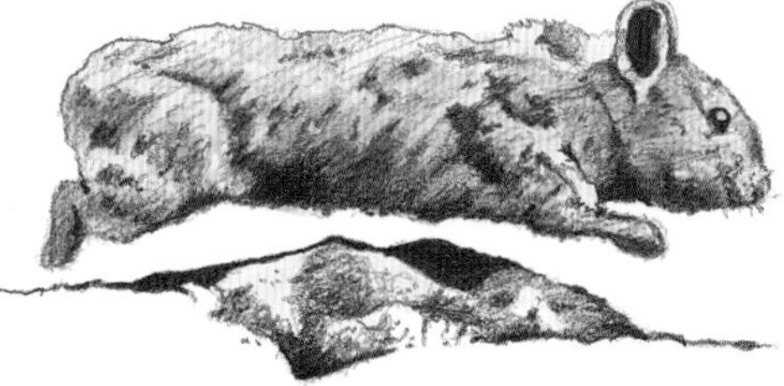

The weasel's claws slashed down, grabbing just where Beejer's tail would have been. If he'd had one. Beejer fell into his own small home. He looked at his smooth, round behind for the tail that wasn't.

Taking a deep, deep breath, he closed his eyes. He was safe.

Early the next day, Beejer sat upon his rock. The sky was blue and there was work to do. But Beejer had something on his mind. He lifted his head high in the air and called as loudly as he could: "BEEEEEJE! BEEEEEEEEJE!" He was saying goodbye to the Tails. He was very glad indeed that they were lost.

The weasel had a tail, the marmot had a tail, and as far as Beejer was concerned, they could keep them.

T H E E N D

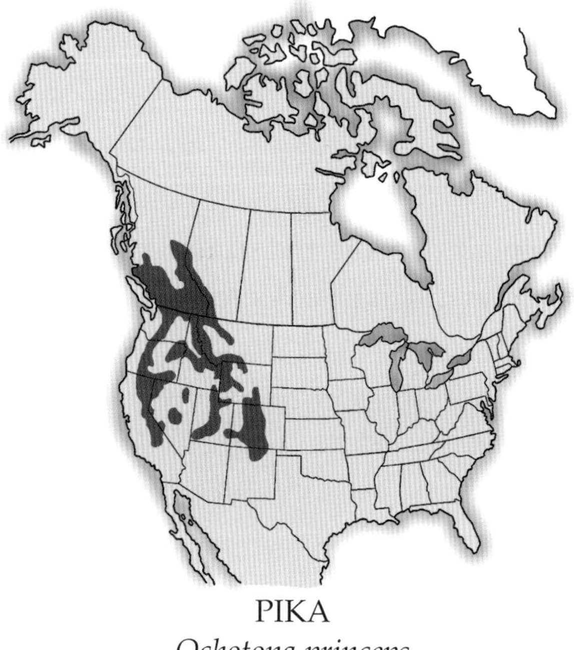

PIKA
Ochotona princeps

COLLARED PIKA
Ochotona collaris

PIKA

The pika, also known as a rock rabbit, coney and Little Chief Hare, leads a busy life. Breeding occurs in May and early June, leading to a gestation period of only thirty days. A litter (average number of three young) is weaned between two and four weeks and a second litter can be born the same season. Newborns weigh only about one ounce, are naked and helpless and are laid in a nest of dried grass. They reach full-size (about that of a guinea pig) at six or seven weeks. Adult pikas have gray-brown fur, round ears and—no tail. They prefer to live amid rock slides and talus slopes, usually high in the mountains.

Pikas eat grasses, forbs, woody twigs and their own soft scats (a source of essential vitamins and nutrients). Rather than hibernate, they create and store hay piles up to three feet in diameter to feast on during the cold winter months.

The pika is more often heard than seen. Its loud, shrill cry frequently protects its territory and warns against enemies such as owls, hawks, martens, coyotes and, of course, weasels.

WEASEL

A weasel is a solitary and fierce hunter. It eats pikas, mice, rabbits, birds, eggs, frogs and other small animals. During the summer, a weasel is brown with a buff-colored belly and white chin. It sports a black-tipped tail which is nearly half its body length of thirteen to eighteen inches. In winter, weasels turn completely white except for the tips of their tails. Active at all hours, in all seasons, the weasel lives in forests and grassy meadows, usually near water.

LONG-TAILED WEASEL
Mustela frenata

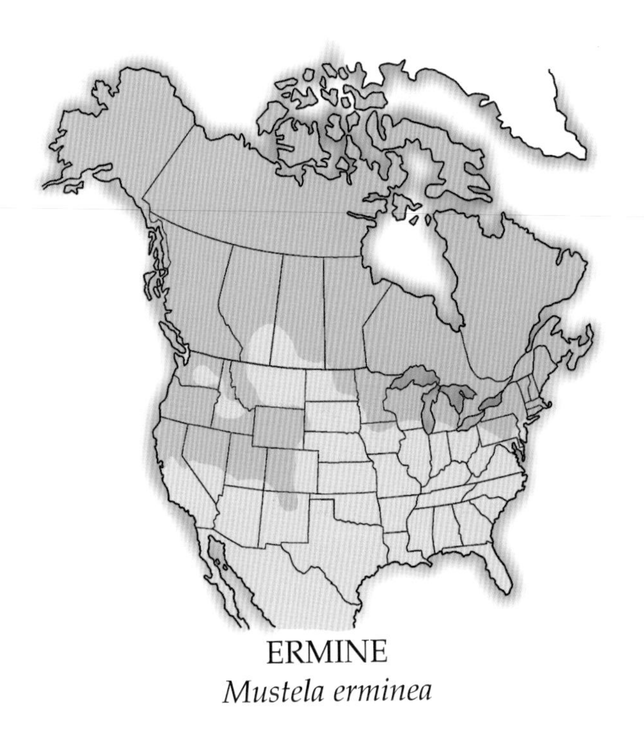

ERMINE
Mustela erminea

MARMOT

A sharp whistle often indicates the presence (and displeasure) of a marmot. Also known as a "rock-chuck," marmots may be found in areas where large boulders and rock slides are intermingled with mountain meadows. Marmots spend considerable time outside of their underground dens feasting on a variety of wildflowers and alpine grasses. They often double in weight in preparation for hibernation that may last from September to March.

Marmots are social animals with reddish-brown fur and a yellowish underside. They are approximately two feet in length and weigh between six to ten pounds. Marmots eat grasses, forbs, seeds and occasionally, insects. In turn, they are a favorite food of coyotes, badgers, bobcats and eagles.

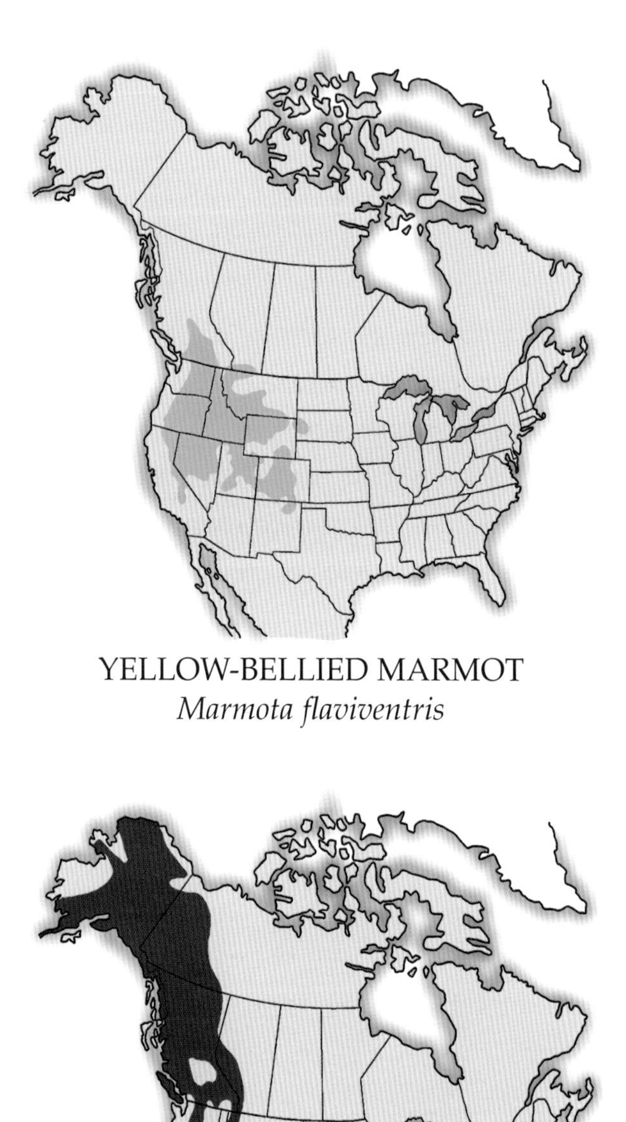

YELLOW-BELLIED MARMOT
Marmota flaviventris

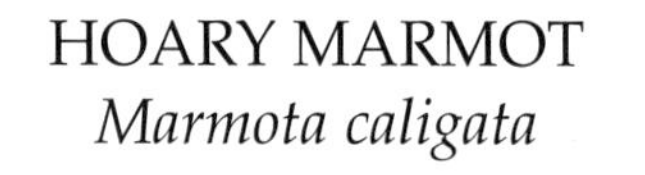

HOARY MARMOT
Marmota caligata

MULE DEER
Odocoileus hemionus

MULE DEER

Mule deer range from mountains to prairies and adapt readily to changes in environment and diet. The "muley" eats over 600 different species of plants including grasses, tree branches, sagebrush and juniper. A mule deer is often identified by its distinct style of running and jumping as all four legs leave the ground and come down at once. They can reach speeds of up to 35 miles per hour.

Mule deer are a reddish-brown color in summer and a gray flecked camouflage color in winter. They have large oversized ears (hence their name) and a black-tipped tail. Male deer (bucks) sport symmetrical antlers. They may leave marks on small trees by rubbing their antlers against the bark and by browsing on twigs and branches. Mule deer are a chief source of food for cougars, bobcats and coyotes.

ABOUT THE AUTHOR

Sally grew up near Evergreen, Colorado on her great-grandfather's Rocky Mountain homestead. She spent summers in the Teton, Gros Ventre and Absaroka mountains of Wyoming, living in the isolated field camps of her geologist father. During college, Sally worked as a seasonal wilderness guard in the Cloud Peak Primitive Area of the Bighorn National Forest, Wyoming. It was through these experiences that she grew to respect and enjoy pikas. Sally met her future husband, Glenn, when he also came to Wyoming to work for the U.S. Forest Service. Their lengthy courtship endured prolonged separations as Sally entered graduate school in Environmental Interpretation and Glenn lived in the Wyoming Red Desert studying wild horse ecology. After marriage, they managed a South Dakota prairie preserve and a research station in Grand Teton National Park, Wyoming. Home is currently Badlands National Park, South Dakota, where Sally is a full-time mother and a volunteer for the park. She continues to enjoy the wonder and beauty of the out-of-doors through work, art and play.

ABOUT THE ARTIST

To prepare for his work on this book, illustrator Lawrence Ormsby spent a summer among pikas on the talus slopes of Grand Teton National Park. He watched and photographed as they went about their lives—dashing from rock to rock, gathering food for the winter, perching on boulders to keep an eye on their territory. The time he spent with pikas gave him a new appreciation of these smallest members of the rabbit family. "To draw an animal and capture its essence, you must study it and learn from it. It's the subtle details of its behavior which are most interesting." When winter came, the pikas retreated to their rocky dens and Lawrence returned to his studio to spend five months completing the illustrations in this book.

Other books illustrated by Larry Ormsby are *Survivors in the Shadows, Threatened and Endangered Mammals of the American West* by Gary Turbak, and *Pueblo Birds and Myths* by Hamilton Tyler. He is creating wildlife images for another children's book by Sally Plumb, *The Hole Story*, about the ecology of black-footed ferrets.

The illustrator would like to thank Grand Teton Natural History Association and their publisher and Executive Director, Sharlene Milligan, for support, inspiration and guidance. Thanks to Lorna Miller, Don Albrecht, and River Meadows for their generosity and patronage during this project. Thanks, Louise Gignoux for guiding the artist to haystacks, alpine flowers and the long-tailed weasel. Thanks also to Tom Mangelsen and Kathy Watkins for sharing their photographic research for four of the weasel drawings.